WINTER
Tales

ISBN 978-0-545-32577-6

12 11 10 9 8 7 6 5 4 3 2 1   11 12 13 14 15 16/0

Printed in the U.S.A.   40
First Scholastic printing, December 2011

WINTER
Tales

Illustrated by Alison Edgson

SCHOLASTIC INC.

New York   Toronto   London   Auckland
Sydney   Mexico City   New Delhi   Hong Kong

CONTENTS

CONTENTS

THE COOLEST
POLAR BEAR

Michael Broad

My name is Arthur and I am a polar bear cub. I live at the North Pole with my mom and tons of other animals, like foxes and seals and wolves and hares. The North Pole is at the top of the world, and of all the animals living here, I think polar bears are the coolest.

We polar bears live inside snowy burrows and can swim in the icy cold ocean because we have very thick fur to keep us warm. We are completely white except for our black noses, and if we don't want to be seen in the snow, we can put a paw on our nose and become invisible!

The North Pole is not just home to animals. There's also a man who lives here with lots of elves and some reindeer. Unlike polar bears, he is very easy to spot in the snow because he always wears red and jingles when he walks. The man's name is Santa Claus.

One morning when I was going out to play, Mom told me that I should not bother the man in red today.

She explained that it was Christmas Eve and that he would be very busy making wishes come true for children all around the world.

"How does he make wishes come true?" I asked.

"I have no idea," said Mom. "Christmas is for humans and has nothing to do with us."

Now, polar bears are very curious animals, and I thought that making wishes come true would be very interesting to see. So I put a paw on my nose and went over the hill to see Santa and his elves and his reindeer. Mom only said that I should not *bother* him, but because

I was invisible, no one saw me peeping through the window of his workshop.

Santa Claus was busy reading letters from a sack and making lists, which was a little boring to watch. The elves were busy wrapping up toys and writing labels, which was not very exciting, either. The reindeer were busy munching loudly on turnips. So no one heard me trudge back home with a disappointed sigh.

Making wishes come true is not as interesting as it sounds.

Back over the hill there seemed to be something *very* interesting happening, though, because all the local animals were gathered at the edge of the ice. I ran up to my mom and asked her what was going on.

"There you are, Arthur!" she said excitedly. "You're just in time for the penguins!"

"What's a penguin?" I asked.

"Penguins are birds that live at the South Pole," Mom explained. "The South Pole is on the other side of the world, but they come here once a year on vacation. They're always a lot of fun to watch."

When Mom said penguins were birds, I looked up in the sky, but I couldn't see anything. I asked if penguins were sky colored with black beaks, so that when they put a wing over their beak they become invisible.

"No, darling." Mom chuckled, and pointed out toward the ocean.

It was then that I saw my first penguin, followed by another and another. Soon there were tons of penguins coming over the horizon, leaping into the air, then diving back into the waves as they swam toward us.

When they reached the ice, the penguins shot out of the water like black-and-white acrobats, landing upright in the snow, and then flapping the water from their flippers. Everyone cheered and welcomed the penguins back to the North Pole, but I was too amazed to say anything.

Mom explained that the penguins like to come to the North Pole because the slopes are smoother than at the South Pole, and that penguins like nothing more than snow-surfing.

"What's snow-surfing?" I asked.

"You'll see," Mom said, as the strange new visitors waddled up the hill.

The penguins put on an amazing show for everyone, zooming down the slopes on their bellies and sideways on their feet. And when they hit the edge of the ice they did backflips and front flips before splashing into the ocean.

It was then that I decided penguins were even *cooler* than polar bears!

When the show was over, I waited until the other animals went home, and then asked the penguins if they could teach me how to snow-surf. They were very friendly, and showed me how to run and launch onto my belly.

But no matter how hard I tried, I was just too big and furry to move very fast. I had to kick my legs the whole way down the slope, and by the time I reached the edge of the ice I just plopped into the water.

I tried for hours and hours, but I still couldn't snow-surf. Then Mom called me in for dinner, so I said good-bye to my new friends and plodded home feeling very unhappy.

"What's the matter, darling?" Mom asked. "You've hardly touched your fish."

"I wish I was a penguin," I said. "Penguins are *much* cooler than polar bears!"

"I'm afraid polar bears can't become penguins, Arthur."

"I guess not," I sighed.

I went to bed early that night, but I couldn't get to sleep. I kept thinking about the penguins and how awesome it must be to surf on the snow. Then I remembered that it was still Christmas Eve, the night that Santa Claus granted wishes!

Mom had said that this special

night was just for human children, but I was sure Santa wouldn't mind granting a wish for one little polar bear cub. So I crept out of bed, left the burrow, and set off for his workshop.

The northern lights lit up the sky in waves of pink and green as I made my way across the snow. When I reached the top of the hill, I saw the reindeer tethered to a large sleigh outside Santa's workshop. The sleigh was filled with presents, and Santa Claus was climbing into his seat at the front!

I bounded down the hill as fast as I could, as Santa took the reins and the reindeer eagerly shook their antlers. I even called out to him, but he couldn't hear me over the sound of sleigh bells ringing in the air.

I knew the only way I'd reach the sleigh in time was if I surfed like a penguin, so I launched myself belly-first onto the snow. But my legs got in the way and I tumbled head over tail down the slope, and when I finally rolled to a stop I was a great big snowball!

I quickly shook off the snow to find I was alone.

Looking up, I could see Santa's sleigh flying through the night sky, soaring through the northern lights with silver stars twinkling in its path.

It was a wonderful sight, but it meant I couldn't tell Santa my wish.

"Christmas is for human children and has nothing to do with polar bears." I sighed.

I was about to go home again when I realized that none of the human children had come to the North Pole to tell Santa their wishes. Which meant the letters I'd seen him reading must have been from them!

So before I left, I crept into the workshop and wrote Santa a letter myself.

Dear Santa Claus,
I am a polar bear
and I wish I was a penguin.
Can you make my wish come true?
Thank you,
Arthur
P.S. I hope you don't mind that I used your paper and pencil.

The next morning I leaped out of bed feeling very excited to begin my first day as a penguin. But when I looked down I saw a white, fluffy belly and white, furry legs, and I still had paws and not flippers. I lifted a paw to my face, but instead of a beak I found a familiar black nose.

"Polar bears just can't become penguins," I sighed.

"Arthur!" Mom called from outside our burrow. "Arthur, come quick!"

When I climbed outside, Mom was standing beside a tall package wrapped in red paper, and she was scratching her head. The penguins were gathered around, too, and they all looked just as bewildered.

Mom gasped. "It says *To Arthur the Polar Bear* on the label."

I stepped up to the box and tore off a small piece of paper, followed by another and another. Then, being a curious polar bear, I couldn't help ripping the rest away all at once. But when the package was unwrapped, I still didn't know what it was until the penguins began clapping their flippers excitedly.

"What is it?" I asked, peering up at the tall, blue object sticking out of the snow.

"It's a surfboard!" cheered the penguins.

I'd never seen a surfboard before, but it didn't take long for me to figure out how to use it. And with the help of the penguins, I spent all of Christmas Day zooming down the slopes!

I started off on my belly, and then learned how to stand up sideways, and I even learned how to do front flips and backflips into the ocean!

Being a polar bear was pretty cool again, and being a polar bear with a surfboard was even cooler. I still think penguins are amazingly cool, but the coolest of all is *definitely* Santa Claus!

REINDEER GIRL

Julia Green

Inga stared out the window into the snowy darkness. "When will Papa get back?" she called to her mom.

"He won't be long now!" Mom came to the kitchen doorway. Her face was red and hot from the stove. "Come and help me make Christmas cookies."

Inga climbed down from the window seat. She was fed up with waiting and watching for Papa to come home. He had gone to get Grandma for Christmas. He should have been back hours ago.

It was only the early afternoon, but in the middle of winter in the Arctic North, it is dark all day as well as all night. Inga was used to it, just as she was used to it being light all day and all night in the summertime. In the spring and summer months, Inga made the long journey with her family and their reindeer herds to the islands off the coast. In the winter months, they lived in their snug little house on the outskirts of the town.

The house was close to the forest, where the reindeer herd grazed on the moss and lichen underneath the soft snow. On days like today, when the snow and ice froze solid, the reindeer couldn't reach the lichen and moss, so Inga and her father took hay for them to eat.

Inga rolled out the cookie dough. She cut out star and heart shapes and put them carefully on the baking sheet.

Mom slid the tray into the hot oven. "When they are cooked, we will thread them with ribbon, and hang them on the birch branch," she said.

Inga and Mom made paper

snowflakes next, to hang up for Christmas decorations. Baby Lars watched Inga. He cooed and babbled and waved his star-shaped hands. Everything was ready for Christmas now. Mom put candles on the table, ready for the special Christmas Eve supper.

Inga went to the window again. Papa and Grandma still hadn't come! The wind howled and whistled around the house, like a wolf trying to get in. But it couldn't. Inga was glad the walls and windows were so tight and solid. Not like the summer tents, the *lavvu*, that they lived in during their long journey in the summertime.

Inga held baby Lars up so he could see out the window, too. He pointed at the long icicles hanging down from the roof and laughed. It began to snow again, small icy flakes that made a noise like pebbles against the window glass.

"I can't think what's taking them so long!" Mom said. She stirred the stew on the stove, ready for supper. "If Papa isn't back soon, you will have to take the hay to the reindeer by yourself today, Inga."

Mom helped Inga pull on her fur-lined reindeer-skin boots, and her fur coat with a big collar, and her fur hat with ear flaps. Finally, Inga put on the beautiful red mittens that Grandma had made for her last Christmas. She was snug and ready for work! Inga had helped look after the reindeer herd ever since she was a tiny girl. She even had four reindeer of her own, each with a special mark cut into its ear.

Mom picked up Lars and opened the door for Inga. She handed her a big, warm shawl to wrap around herself in the sleigh. Inga walked the short distance to the barn. She turned to wave, and Mom went back into the house. It was too cold outside for baby Lars today.

Inside the barn it smelled of sweet, dry hay and the strong scent of animals. They kept the tame reindeer in the barn, ready to pull the sleighs or for riding. The reindeer stamped their hooves on the barn floor, and jostled their big antlers. They pushed their soft brown muzzles forward for Inga to pet them.

"Hello, Sky," Inga said to her favorite reindeer. She patted Sky's rough, furry neck and scratched the creamy fur on her head between her antlers. Sky liked that.

Inga put the harness around Sky's neck and filled the sleigh with hay. She hitched Sky up to the sleigh, and led her out of the barn. Inga knew exactly what to do since she had helped Papa so many times. Inga was proud of knowing all the Sami ways of working with reindeer.

"Let's go!" Inga shook the reins and Sky started to trot. Sky's job was to take her to the place in the forest where the herd was sheltering. Sky knew just where to go. Her hooves gripped perfectly, and the sleigh's runners slid easily over the fresh snow.

Inga heard the reindeer before she

could see them in the darkness. They were like a heaving sea, pawing at the snow and snorting and rattling their antlers with one another. They were hungry.

"Whoa, Sky!" Inga pulled on the reins and Sky stopped and lowered her head, so the bells on the harness jingled.

The reindeer crowded around as Inga scattered armfuls of hay for them. They pulled at it with their soft mouths.

"There! All done!" Inga climbed onto the sleigh again. "Back home, Sky!"

It was snowing again. Inga pulled

her hat down and wrapped the shawl tight around her face, leaving only a space for her eyes. The wind was freezing.

She thought about Papa for the millionth time that day. Maybe he was taking so long because something had happened. What if Grandma was ill? Or Papa had run out of fuel for the snowmobile? What if they were stuck somewhere, broken down?

"Let's go and look for Papa," Inga said out loud. "Go to Grandma's house, Sky."

The reindeer slowed to a walk. Her ears twitched, as if she was listening.

In the distance, Inga could see the lights of the town. They were almost home. She pulled sharply on the rein in her right hand, to make Sky turn in the other direction.

Sky trotted faster again. She understood. She had been to Grandma's house many times before.

The snow fell faster. It was so cold, so dark. Inga's toes were snug in her fur-lined boots, but her fingers were cold, her nose was like ice, and her eyes stung. The wind seemed stronger and wilder, tugging at her. Inga started to feel scared. What if she was going in the wrong direction? What if Sky was taking her out onto the snowy plains, in the middle of nowhere? The air was full of white, swirling snow-feathers.

Inga felt sleepy, sitting still while Sky pulled the sleigh along. She knew she must not fall asleep in the cold. She clapped her hands together to warm them up. She started to sing one of the songs that Grandma had taught her, a song to the snow:

"The snow is cold, but also a blanket . . ."

She sang another song for Sky, her special reindeer:

"Swift and strong, you run all day
In the thickest blizzard you find the way . . ."

Singing out loud in the middle of the blizzard made Inga feel stronger and braver. She sang as loud as she could.

And suddenly Inga heard something else, besides the soft *thud, thud* of Sky's hooves and the swish of the sleigh runners and the whistle of the wind. Another voice was singing out the exact same words as Inga!

"The snow is cold, but also a blanket . . ."

Inga's heart beat faster. She knew that voice! It was Grandma's! She strained forward, peering through the snow and the darkness. Was that a light ahead?

Sky's pace slowed down. Her ears pricked up.

"Inga?" Papa's voice! "What on earth are you doing here?"

"I heard your song," Grandma said. "What a lovely surprise!"

"What happened to you?" Inga asked. She climbed down from the sleigh.

Papa hugged her tight. "I drove the snowmobile right into a big drift, by mistake. It is really and truly stuck. I tried shoveling the snow, but I still couldn't move it. Now that you are here, we can hitch up a rope to the reindeer and pull the snowmobile out. Poor Grandma's gotten very cold."

"Nonsense!" Grandma said. "I'm fine. But didn't I always say, Inga, that the old ways are the best? A reindeer would never get stuck in snow like that silly machine! New technology? Hah!"

Papa laughed. He heaved and shoved the snowmobile, and Inga and Grandma helped, and Sky pulled the rope. Together, little by little, they freed it from the snowdrift.

Grandma tucked herself under her special fur blanket in the sleigh. Inga gave Sky a handful of hay to eat, and then climbed up and snuggled next to Grandma under the blanket. She picked up the

reins and
they began
the journey
home. Papa
followed them on
the snowmobile.

At last, Inga saw the faint lights of
the town in the distance, and then
the light from the windows of their
own house, shining out over the
snow. There was the barn!

Mom was already opening the
door, running out to hug Inga and
hold her tight. "I was worried!"
she said.

Grandma told her what had happened. "Inga and Sky came to the rescue," she said. "I don't know what we'd have done without them."

Papa helped Inga unhitch the sleigh. Inga led Sky back into the barn. She fed her dried lichen, and rubbed the creamy fur on her head.

Sky looked as tired as Inga felt!

Inside the warm house, Mom helped Inga pull off her boots and coat and hat and mittens. Lars gurgled and waved his little hands. The candles on the table shone bright.

"Supper's ready! Sit up at the table, everyone!" Mom ladled hot, spicy stew into bowls.

Papa thanked the reindeer spirits for the precious gifts of food and family.

Grandma smiled at Inga. "And a special thank-you to Sky and Inga," she said.

Inga looked at everyone around the table: Grandma and Papa and Mom and Lars, all happy and smiling and warm in the little winter house. She looked at the paper snowflakes hanging from the birch branches in the corner of the room, and the piles of presents underneath. Outside was the snow blizzard and the cold and darkness, but inside all was snug and cozy and safe.

"Now," Grandma said, "time for a story, and a song, and then off to bed. Tomorrow it will be Christmas Day!"

But before Inga had heard more than the first words of the story, she was already drifting asleep.

"Once upon a time, a reindeer girl was staring out into the snowy darkness . . ."

MIA AND
THE LOST
PENGUIN

Holly Webb

"I'm so sorry you can't come, Mia."
Mom tucked the covers around
me gently. "Dad will take care of
you, though. Just call if you need
anything, okay?"

I made a gaspy, rattling noise—
that was all I could manage at the
moment.

"Well, just thump on the floor,
and he'll hear that." Mom looked
down at me worriedly, but then my
big sister, Sophie, yelled up the stairs.

"Mom, we'll be late! The theater won't let us in if we're not there on time!" Mom gave me an apologetic smile and hurried out, leaving me sniffing miserably.

It was so unfair. It was Christmas Eve, I had the world's worst cold, and I was missing our special Christmas treat, going to see *The Nutcracker*. I love ballet, and I'd been looking forward to it for a long time. But I couldn't really sit in the theater coughing and blowing my nose and distracting everyone from the wonderful story and the dancing and the costumes—oh, it was just so unfair!

Mom had said to try and sleep, but I didn't feel tired. She'd left tons of new books from the library, and Sophie had even loaned me the TV from her bedroom, but I didn't feel like that, either.

I was too miserable. I flopped over onto my side, grumbling as I coughed again, and hugged Ferdie, my old stuffed toy penguin. I've had him since I was about two, and he's my favorite. I love penguins—I have tons of posters of them, and I was even wearing my blue, fluffy penguin pajamas.

"You all right, Mia?" Dad stuck his head around the door.

"It started to snow, look! We're going to have a white Christmas!"

I wriggled up onto my elbow and peered out the window. He was right. Fat, lazy snowflakes were floating down against a dark gray sky. It had been so cold that the snow was bound to stick. Great. All my friends would be out making snowmen on Christmas Day, and I'd be stuck inside, if Mom even let me get out of bed.

As I lay there dreamily watching the whirling snowflakes with Ferdie tucked under my arm, it got colder and colder. At first I thought it was just because I could see the snow falling and it was making me feel cold, but then I realized I could see my breath puffing out in front of me. I sat up, pulling my covers around my shoulders like a big, warm cloak.

Then, suddenly, Ferdie wriggled under my arm, his gray feathers silky soft. I looked down in amazement, and he gazed back shyly with his bright, beady eyes, his head to one side. Then he wriggled out of the covers, and hopped clumsily down onto snow, still looking back at me as though he wasn't quite sure what I was.

I shook myself, trying to wake up. I had to be dreaming. I still had my blue penguin pajamas on, and I was all wrapped up in my covers, but my bedroom had disappeared. Instead, I was in the middle of a snowfield, surrounded by white as far as I could see.

I stared around, blinking at the brightness of the shining snow. The wind was shrieking in my ears, and flurries of snowflakes swirled around me, making me shiver. It looked as though a storm was just blowing over. I glanced over my shoulder and gasped—huge, snow-covered mountains were rising behind us, back where I'd mistakenly thought my bedroom would be waiting. I shook my head slowly, and took a deep breath of freezing cold air. Meanwhile, Ferdie was waddling clumsily away across the whiteness.

"Hey! Stop!" I jumped up, not wanting to lose the only thing I knew in this strange world, and Ferdie looked back at me hopefully. He waggled his flipper, as if to tell me to hurry up, and kept on lurching across the hard-packed snow. I followed him, skidding and sliding, and tripping over my blanket.

"This has to be a dream," I murmured, looking down at my bare feet stepping over the Antarctic snow. "If it was real, my feet would probably have turned blue and fallen off by now. . . ."

Ferdie seemed anxious. It was clear that he wasn't just going for a walk—he was trying to get somewhere. He was only a chick, and he shouldn't really be out on his own—he should be with his parents or the other penguin chicks. I guessed he must have wandered away in the snowstorm and gotten lost.

He was hopping and bouncing over the bumpy ground, flapping his funny little flippers for balance. But he didn't seem to be very good at it—he kept falling over, even though his little black feet had sharp claws to help him grip. I couldn't help giggling. He looked so funny! He was so fat and furry, with his little black-and-white head bobbing around on top of his gray, fluffy body.

But after the third fall, I stopped laughing, or even wanting to. Ferdie could hardly get up. He seemed so tired, and he just lay down in the snow. His bright, beady eyes looked back at me sadly, and then he closed them, and he didn't move.

I caught up with Ferdie and crouched down beside him. "Ferdie! Ferdie, wake up! You can't sleep here!" I looked around worriedly. "You'll freeze." *I* was cold, and I was only a dream-person, not even really there. Ferdie might have all that beautiful fluff, but I was pretty sure it wouldn't keep him warm for very long if he just lay there in the snow.

Ferdie's eyes flickered open for a moment and he gave a sad little sigh, but then they closed again. They hadn't been as bright and shiny this time—they were starting to look misted over. Ferdie was giving up.

Gently I reached out to pet him. I cuddled my toy Ferdie all the time, but this Ferdie was real, and he was wild. I didn't want to scare him. Ferdie hardly even moved when I brushed his soft feathers with my hand. Tears dripped out of the corners of my eyes, and I felt them freezing on my cheeks.

"Don't give up, Ferdie, please!"

I whispered. And, hoping that I wasn't doing the wrong thing, I scooped him up in my arms.

He was a lot heavier than my toy penguin, and bigger. He smelled like fish. He wriggled a little, as though he didn't think someone should be cuddling him, but then he didn't move.

Clumsily, still dragging my covers—I didn't want to let go of them since they felt like my only piece of home—I trailed on. Ferdie had been following a straight path. If I looked back, I could see the marks of his shuffling feet, although I hadn't left any footprints at all—I suppose dream-people don't. So I tried to keep on going in the same sort of line. Ferdie seemed to get heavier with every step I took.

At last, we came to a little rise in the snowfield, and I dragged my way slowly up it. Then I gasped. Stretched out on the ice in front of me were thousands and thousands of penguins. They were emperor penguins, I could tell, because they had black heads with orange patches on the sides. That strange noise I had thought was the wind was the penguins calling to each other—loud sounds, almost like donkeys braying.

I was so excited to see them that I accidentally hugged Ferdie tight, and he made a funny little upset noise. At least he was starting to wake up. My cuddling him and making him warm again must have helped.

Then I had a horrible thought. This was Ferdie's home, but there were at least two thousand penguins here! Which ones did he belong to? "Oh, Ferdie," I muttered to the fluffy bundle tucked inside my blanket. "I'm sure this is where you wanted to get to. But I don't know how you're going to find your mom or dad."

Ferdie was wriggling now. He popped his little black head out of the covers and stared around eagerly, his eyes bright and alert. He tried to flap his flippers, and I guessed he wanted to get down, so I placed him gently on the ice, wondering sadly what he was going to do. The penguins all looked alike to me, and there were hundreds of other fluffy gray chicks, too.

Ferdie waddled down the little slope determinedly, and started to rock his head backward and forward, calling loudly. I could barely hear him, though, because all the other chicks were doing the same, shouting, "Piu! Piu!" again and again, louder and louder every time, and their parents were hastily trying to feed them.

I looked around, wondering if any of the other penguins would be kind enough to give Ferdie some food, but they were all focused on their own chicks. Poor Ferdie. He'd come so far, but he was still all alone.

Then, suddenly an enormous penguin barged

past me, heading straight for Ferdie. He was one of the tallest ones I'd seen—he came up to my waist and he nearly knocked me over. He *did* knock Ferdie over, but obviously because he was so excited to see his lost chick. He nudged him up right away, snuggled him into his tummy feathers, and started feeding him.

I was colder again without Ferdie to cuddle, so I sat down to wrap myself in my covers. It was so cold, I began to feel sleepy. The snow was falling again, those same big fat flakes that had been outside my window at home. I wondered how I was going to get back there. *But at least I rescued Ferdie,* I thought. *He's home safe. . . .*

"Hey, Mia. . . . Time for your medicine, sweetheart." Dad was sitting on my bed, gently shaking me. "Wow, it's chilly in here. I'd better turn the radiator up."

I blinked at him. Wasn't I just in a snowfield full of penguins?

"Were you dreaming, Mia? You look a little dazed." Dad smiled at me as he poured the medicine.

"Mmm." I took a quick look around. This was definitely my room.

And there was Ferdie, on my pillow. Fluffy and snuggly, smiling and safe.

TWO LITTLE
SNOW
LEOPARDS

Caroline Pitcher

In a mountain cave in the land of
Tibet lived two little snow leopards
with their mother. Their names were
Meru and Maya.

Maya rolled over and waved her
big paws in the air. Underneath, they
were thick with fur.

"Why are my feet so big and furry,
Mom?" she cried.

"To help you walk in the deep
snow and to protect your paws from
the cold," said her mother.

"If you think your paws are big,

just look at mine."

"Wow!" squealed the cubs.

Their mother laughed. "Our furry feet are our snowshoes, my beautiful cubs."

"Your tummy is furry, too, Maya," said Meru. "You've got a big, furry belly." He batted her ear with his big paw. "Mom's eyes are iced gold, but yours are sky blue."

Maya squeaked. "You've got sky blue eyes and thick fur, too, you know, Meru. All white, with spots and rings. And it looks like snow clouds are floating across your back."

Their mother looked down at them and said, "Your thick fur will keep you warm. It is pale and dark like the snow and rocks. The mountainside is a snow-leopard landscape and your fur will make you invisible. No one can see you out there. You are two little secrets in the snow."

"Good!" said Meru.

"We're invisible!" squeaked Maya. She swiped at Meru, and the cubs tussled and tumbled until their mother growled softly. "Stop that now," she said. "Let's sleep. I'm going hunting at dawn, and won't be back until nightfall."

"Can we come, too?" chorused the cubs.

"No. I will go alone," she said.

"You are still too young."

"Can we play outside while you're away?"

"Yes. But don't stray too far from the cave. Always be sure you can see the juniper tree that grows outside. Then you won't get lost."

"Silly old juniper tree!" sniffed Meru. "It's just a big stick with prickles and a few shriveled berries."

"It's a special juniper tree because it shows where we live," said their mother. "Now lie still and close your eyes."

Outside, the blue-black night crackled with stars. The moon tipped light down onto the mountainside. In the cave, the cubs slept, with their tails wrapped around themselves like scarves.

At dawn, the mother snow leopard looked at them once with her iced gold eyes and slipped out of the cave alone. The cubs stirred in their sleep as her paws crunched lightly on the snow crust and she vanished into the snow-leopard landscape.

When the cubs awoke, the sky was startling blue and the world was diamond bright.

"C'mon!" squeaked Meru.

"Coming!" squeaked Maya.

They scampered out of the cave

and blinked in the slanting sunshine.

"Look down there," cried Meru.

"Wow!" cried Maya.

They gazed down from the mountain ledge.

A hare was nibbling at the bark of a birch tree. He stopped when he heard the cubs and disappeared down the mountainside.

Below them, Meru and Maya saw bright prayer flags snapping and flapping in the wind. In the valley, big black yaks lumbered along a track and a donkey brayed in the corral near the village.

"That looks fun. Want to go down there?" said Meru.

"No," replied Maya. "Mom said not to stray far from the cave. But look up there. . . . Wow!"

High in the clear sky hovered a golden eagle.

As Meru looked up, Maya put her big paws around her brother's face. "C'mon! Let's play," she cried. "You pretend to be a blue mountain sheep and I'll chase you. Coming, ready or not!"

Wheee! The cubs raced up and down the mountainside, leaping from rock to rock with their tails behind them like sails, sending little avalanches sliding down the slopes to the valley.

Finally, they came to a stop and stood panting for breath, with their pink mouths open and their little sides heaving.

"Phew!" cried Meru. "I'm out of breath. We've come a really long way, Maya."

"Yes, but look at our paw prints in the snow, going all the way to our cave. And I can still see the juniper tree."

"Silly old tree," sniffed Meru. "C'mon! I'll chase you!"

They scampered off, jumping from rock to rock. They butted heads and swiped and pounced and scampered off again, until they stopped, panting. From their noses came little puffs of frozen breath.

"Look at the snow-leopard land," cried Maya. "The mountainside is like Mom's fur, all white with dark rings."

"Tell you what, Maya," said

Meru, "Mom said we were invisible out here, so let's play hide-and-seek. I'll hide first."

He trotted off and lay very still on the snow.

"Coming, ready or not . . ." said Maya. "Hey, Meru?"

"Yes?" he squeaked.

"Found you!" she squealed. "Now it's my turn to hide."

She scampered in and out of the rocks and hid in a crevice. Meru searched for a long time. He padded right past and did not see her. After a while he began to whimper, "It's not fair! I can't see you. Where are you, Maya?"

"Boo!" she cried, pouncing out at him. They chased each other around and around.

"Hey, something dropped on my nose," squeaked Meru.

"And my head is getting wet," said Maya. "It's snowing."

"Let's sled!" squealed Meru, and the cubs playfully slipped and slid down the mountainside.

"I can't see where I'm going now," grumbled Meru. "The snow is flying sideways. I'm tired. I think I'll take a little nap under the shelter of this rock."

"I think I will, too," yawned Maya. "I'm very sleepy."

The cubs curled up and dozed, with

their tails wound around themselves like scarves.

While the cubs slept, the snow fell and fell, and the wind wrapped it around the mountain.

When the cubs woke up, the world was completely changed.

"Just look down there," whispered Meru. "I can't see anything at all."

"Neither can I," whispered Maya. "Maybe that big bird can show us the way back." She blinked up into the sky to find the golden eagle, but she couldn't see anything except swirling snowflakes.

"We'd better go home," she said.

"But where is home?" squeaked

Meru. "I can't see the juniper tree. . . . "

"Let's look for our paw prints," said Maya.

The cubs stared and stared, but so much snow had fallen it had covered up the trail of paw prints. Their tracks had vanished.

"Never mind," said Maya. "Let's sniff and smell where our paws have been, and follow the scent back to the cave."

The cubs sniffed and sniffed, but they could not even find the scent of their own feet. The fresh snow had hidden it.

"Wah! I want to be home and cozy inside the cave with Mom,"

squeaked Meru.

"At least we're invisible in this snow-leopard landscape. Nothing can get us," said Maya.

"But that means Mom won't be able to find us, either," cried Meru. "She won't be able to see us because our coats keep us a secret."

The cubs sat down. They did not know what to do. They just sat, getting colder and wetter.

"You're beginning to look like a pile of snow," squeaked Maya.

"Well, I can't help it. You look like a snowball," snapped Meru.

"Let's not fight," said Maya. "Let's be smart. It will be nighttime soon, and if we fall asleep in the snow again, we will be too cold. We need to search for our juniper tree, and then we'll find home. You go that way and I'll go this way."

"No!" yowled Meru. "I'll get lost. Let's stay together, Maya. I want to find our juniper tree!"

"All right," she said. "Look where we are now. You can tell we've been here from this dip in the snow. So this is our starting place. Come on, Meru."

Maya sighed and set out across the snow with her brother trotting close behind her.

They knew that they must find

that juniper tree. But all they could see was snow, falling around them like thick feathers.

The sky was growing dark. Soon the stars would glitter and the mountain would be colder than ever.

"I'm getting tired," whispered Meru. "But I don't want to have to sleep out here in the cold."

"Me, neither," whispered Maya.

"Can you see the juniper tree yet?" said Meru.

"No," Maya said. "Can you?"

"No," he whimpered. "And I can't go any farther."

"You have to," she cried. "You have to keep going. Soon we'll be cuddled up with Mom in our warm, dry den . . . soon . . . and we'll sleep so cozily . . . Meru?"

Behind her, Meru had stopped. His legs folded under him and he sank down in the snow.

Maya turned and sank down next to him. She nuzzled his ears and said, "Maybe Mom will come and find us."

"She won't be able to see us in the snow-leopard landscape," insisted Meru.

"Maybe she will. Cuddle up close," sighed Maya.

"All right," he mumbled. "But I think someone has already been here and made a dip in the snow. Ow! OW!"

"What?"

"I knocked my head on something. Something prickly. It's . . . it's . . ."

"The juniper tree!" they squealed together, and jumped up again.

"This is where we stopped," cried Maya. "We were next to the tree the whole time and we didn't know it. We're home. And . . . hello, Mom!"

"I am so proud of you both," purred their mother as she approached the cubs. "I was going to come get you, but I waited a moment when I saw that you were finding your own way home like big snow leopards."

"You said we were invisible!" squeaked Meru.

"You said we're two small secrets in our special fur," said Maya.

"So how could you see us out on the mountainside?" squealed Meru.

"Because I am your mother," she purred. "Now, come inside to the warmth on this cold winter night."

Outside, the blue-black night crackled with stars. The moon tipped light down onto the mountainside. In the cave, Maya and Meru cuddled up to their mother and slept, with their tails wrapped around themselves like scarves.

MUSK

Malachy Doyle

"Wake up, child! Come and see!"

Lucy opened her eyes. There was a huge hairy face, *tap-tap-tapping* with one of its long, curvy horns on her bedroom window.

Lucy blinked, not really believing what she saw. It was big, like a cow, but it definitely wasn't a cow. It was woolly, like a sheep, but it wasn't a sheep, either. It had horns, a little like a goat, but Lucy had never seen a goat like this before. *Am I dreaming?* she thought. *Is it real?*

She slid out of bed and opened the window, just a crack. A blast of icy wind hit her in the face. There was a smell, too—a strange and powerful smell.

"Hello," said Lucy. "Who are you?"

"I'm a musk ox," replied the creature. "I've come to show you something."

"I haven't heard of a musk ox," said Lucy, who'd never seen anything quite like him before, not even in the zoo. "Are you lost?"

"No, I'm not lost," replied the

musk ox. "But I've come a long way, from the frozen North—the land of snow and ice—and I need to get back as soon as I can, since it's much too warm for me here."

"Too warm?" repeated Lucy, shivering. "It's freezing, with the window open like that."

"Let me in, then," said the musk ox, "and I'll tell you why I've come."

So Lucy opened the window wide, just for a minute, while the animal clambered through.

"Did I come to the right place?" he asked her, trying to squeeze into the space between the bed and the wall. The room was full of him, and full of his smell, too—a strange, strong, not unpleasant smell, thought Lucy.

"Is your name Lucy?" he asked.

She nodded.

"Do you have a little brother named Joe?"

She nodded again.

"You're proud of him, aren't you?" said the musk ox.

"Very," replied Lucy, who loved her little brother more than anything.

"Well, that's why I came," said the creature.

"What do you mean?" said Lucy, confused.

"To meet you and Joe. And to show you something."

"What sort of something?"

"I can't tell you," said the musk ox. "I have to take you to see, instead. Will you come? You can ride on my back and we'll go there and come home again before dawn."

"I don't know," said Lucy, frowning. "I'm not sure I should."

"It'd be wonderful if you would," said the musk ox, and when Lucy glanced into his eyes, she saw stars and snow, icicles and rainbows. And she knew, just by looking at him, that she and Joe would be safe.

"All right, Mister Musk Ox," she

told him. "Wait here and I'll go and get Joe."

She threw on her slippers and ran to get her little brother. "Joe!" she cried, nudging him from sleep. "Come and see! There's the strangest animal in my bedroom, and he wants to meet you."

"Me?" Joe snuffled.

"Yes, you! He's big, like a cow," said Lucy, "with horns like a goat and all woolly, like a sheep. Come and see, Joe—quick, before he disappears!"

Joe's eyes opened wide then, and he slid out of bed.

"He says he's going to take us on a journey through the night," Lucy whispered, helping her little brother with his slippers. "Here, put these on—it's cold out there. Come and see!"

She tiptoed down the landing, with Joe padding along behind her. But suddenly he turned and rushed back to his bedroom.

"Tom!" he said, grabbing his sailor doll from the pillow. "Come and see, Tom. . . ."

"Ah," said Lucy, smiling when she saw what he was holding. "I'd forgotten about Tom!" Joe never went anywhere without the doll—not even to the bathroom in the middle of the night.

Lucy led him to her room, and even though she'd told Joe what to expect, her little brother gasped when he saw the size of the big musk ox. He wrinkled up his nose, too, when he smelled him.

"Don't be afraid, Joe," said the creature. "I won't hurt you. And if you're happy to fly through the night with me, I'll make sure no harm comes to you."

Joe looked at Lucy, and Lucy looked at Joe.

"We'll come, Mister Musk Ox," said Lucy, clambering over the bed to get past him to the window and open it wide.

"Hold on tight, then," said the animal, and they climbed up onto his back, grabbing hold of his woolliness.

Then, with a mighty swoosh, the musk ox flew out and over the rooftops, out and over the town.

It was the coldest of nights and there was snow all around, but the comfort of his long, brown hair kept Joe and Lucy snug. On they flew, by the light of the winter moon, over cities and farms and hills and seas, and in time, the smell and the warmth of him lulled them to sleep.

"Wake up, you two," cried the musk ox at last. "We're coming in to land!"

The children blinked and then looked all around as they came to rest by a stable.

"Come with me, children," said the animal, leading Joe and Lucy inside.

It was dark in the stable, but there was a small light in the corner. The musk ox led them toward the light, which came from a newborn child, lying in the hay.

"Baby . . ." said Joe, dropping to his knees.

He whispered little Joe-words to the infant, and then remembered the sailor doll he was still clutching in his hand.

"Tom . . ." he said, holding it above the baby's eyes. And the newborn gurgled happily.

"Tom . . ." said Joe again, dangling the little sailor man by one arm and swinging him slowly from side to side.

The baby chuckled, as his eyes followed the movement.

"Baby . . ." said Joe, pressing the doll into the newborn's hand.

The infant clutched his tiny fingers around the precious gift, and then stared up into Joe's eyes and seemed to smile.

"But, Joe . . ." said Lucy, shocked. "You can't give Tom away! He's your one and only! Your favorite!"

"Baby . . ." said Joe, with a smile that was happy and sad. "Good baby."

The musk ox looked at them, unsurprised. "You're very kind, Joe," he said, nodding his heavy head. "This child has just been born, and you're the first person to bring him a present and welcome him into the world."

"Why is the baby's head so bright, Mister Musk Ox?" Lucy asked. "It's like he's on fire or something!"

"It's to tell everyone how special

he is," the animal answered.

"Like Joe?" said Lucy, who was so proud of her little brother.

"Yes," said the creature. "Joe is loving and giving, just as this child will be. And now I must take you both home."

"I want you to do something for me, children," said the musk ox as they climbed up onto his back. "I want you to tell other people you see about the baby. I want you to tell them he has come into the world. Will you do that for me?"

"We will," said Lucy. "Won't we, Joe?"

Her little brother nodded happily.

"The baby's born!" cried Lucy, as they flew through the ice-cold night. "It's Christmas morning and the baby's born!"

"Baby!" cried Joe. "Baby!"

"Where?" came a voice from far below them. "Where is this special baby you speak of? We heard that he was coming, and we have been trying to find him for days."

"In a stable," cried Lucy, pointing. "Over there!"

"Baby!" cried Joe happily.

And the three kings, each with a gift for the newborn child, turned in the direction Lucy pointed, trudging onward through the starlit snow.

Back in Joe and Lucy's town, the Christmas bells rang out as the musk ox helped the children into their beds.

"Where are you going, Mister Musk Ox?" asked Lucy drowsily. He was outside the window now, pulling it shut with one of his horns.

"Home to the frozen North," whispered the great, lumbering creature. "My job is done here. Merry Christmas, Lucy."

"Merry Christmas," murmured Lucy, pulling the covers tight around her. "Thank you for taking us to see the baby."

In the morning, when Joe and Lucy woke up, there were presents waiting for them. The present Joe liked best was a small wooden animal, with hair nearly to the ground, and long, curly horns.

And the one Lucy liked best was in a tiny blue box. She took off the ribbon, opened the box, and there inside was a little green bottle.

When she eased open the stopper, out came a smell that filled the whole room. It was a smell of sweetness and spice, of animal, earth, and baby.

And when she looked at the label on the front of the bottle, she smiled at the single word that was written there: "Musk."

THE MIDWINTER MAGIC SHOW

Karen Wallace

Gordon was a young grizzly bear who lived in the far, far North where winter went on for months and months. Sometimes, when the other bears were dozing or just watching the snowflakes come down, Gordon closed his eyes and dreamed his favorite dream.

Gordon's dream was to be a magician. Not just any magician. Gordon wanted to be a really good magician so that in the middle of winter, when it was coldest and darkest, he could put on a show for all the other animals and make them happy.

"Don't be crazy," said Gordon's big sister, Gabby. "You're a grizzly bear. You can't be a magician. You're too big and too clumsy. Besides, you don't know any tricks."

Gordon looked at his sister with his bright, clever eyes. She was the one who was big and clumsy. What's more, all she ever thought about was food. Especially in the winter when it was hard to find any. Every night in their cave, Gabby kept him awake with her sleep-talking.

Snakes, fish, frogs, birds, insects, honey.
Honey, honey, honey.

"I can *learn* tricks," said Gordon. "Mom will teach me."

"Don't be crazy," said Gabby again. "Mom teaches us what grizzly bears do. Like catching fish when the ice melts and finding moss under the snow. What would she know about magic tricks?"

Gabby stuffed some dry berries left over from the summer into her big, red mouth. "You're sthtupid," she said as she chomped them up. Then she waddled away, leaving a trail of paw prints in the snow.

Gordon stared after his sister.

Sometimes he wished she would be nice to him. Just once. But maybe that's what big sisters were like.

"It sounds like you have a problem." A squirrel cocked his head and looked down from a branch high above Gordon. It wasn't that the squirrel, whose name was Simon, didn't trust Gordon. They'd known each other since they were both little. But Gordon was a grizzly bear, and even good friends can forget their manners sometimes.

Gordon slumped to the ground and leaned back against the trunk of the tree. A big dollop of snow fell on his head. "I want to be a magician," he said.

Simon crept a little nearer. "So, what's wrong with that? You can be whatever you want."

"Gabby says I'm crazy," said Gordon.

"*She's* the crazy one," said Simon firmly. "She tried to eat me yesterday! Me! How *could* she?"

"No manners, and all she thinks about is food," said Gordon. "She's probably jealous of all those acorns you've got hidden in your nest." He shook the snow from his head. "Even so, she shouldn't have done that. I'll tell my mom."

"Don't bother," said Simon. "*She* tried to eat me the day before."

Gordon slumped down even farther and put his head in his paws. This time he didn't bother to rub off the snow that fell on his head.

"Sorry," said Simon. "I didn't mean to make things worse. In fact, I was going to give you a tip." He tapped his head with his tiny paw. "Squirrels know a thing or two."

"What do you mean?"

"An enormous owl with eyes like yellow plates has moved into the dead tree by the big, black rock," said Simon.

"So?"

"So, everyone says there's nothing that owl doesn't know," said Simon. "Apparently he's one of those *really* wise snowy owls that come from the North Pole."

Gordon had never heard of such owls.

"Do you think he might teach me how to be a magician?" he asked.

"Why not?" asked Simon.

Gordon jumped up so quickly that Simon almost fell off his branch.

He always forgot how fast grizzly bears could move.

"Thanks, Simon!" cried Gordon. "You're a *real* pal!"

Ten minutes later, Gordon stood underneath the dead tree by the big, black rock. He stood up on his hind legs and scratched at the bark.

An enormous owl appeared from a hole above him. He blinked his huge, yellow eyes and shook some snowflakes off his white, feathery ears. "It's early for me to be up," he said.

"Sorry to disturb you," said Gordon shyly. "But—"

"Ah yes, you're the young grizzly that wants to be a magician," interrupted Wise Owl, yawning. "Well, what can I do for you?"

Gordon was so surprised, his mouth opened but no words came out. "Can you teach me how to do magic tricks?" he said at last.

"No," replied Wise Owl. "But I do have a book you can borrow and a wand you can keep."

He disappeared into his tree and came out with a blue book under his wing and a wand in his beak. The book was called *Magic Tricks:*

The Bear Facts. He dropped them in the snow beside Gordon's feet.

"Now all you need is a cloak and top hat," said Wise Owl.

"Where will I find those?" asked Gordon.

Wise Owl hooted with laughter. "Your mother will know," he said.

Gordon ran back to where his mother was dozing in her cave. In the winter, she spent most of her time asleep.

Sure enough, Wise Owl was right. Gordon's mom muttered about terrible indigestion, and then something about a traveling circus that had gotten lost in the woods many years before.

She pointed toward the back of the cave. Under a pile of leaves, there was an old top hat and a cloak.

For the next week, Gordon taught himself magic tricks. Soon he could make a bunch of flowers appear out of his paws and pull shiny pebbles out from behind his friends' ears.

All the other animals thought he was amazing.

Except for his sister, Gabby.

"Who wants flowers and shiny pebbles in the middle of winter?" Gabby took a deep breath. "We want snakes, fish, frogs, birds, insects, and honey. Especially honey. Anyway, you can't be a *real* magician if you don't have a rabbit."

The other animals stopped and stared. All the talk about food had made them hungry and irritated.

"She's right," said an old moose.

"Can't say it better than that," growled a gray wolf.

"Gordon's not a magician! Gordon's not a magician!" squealed a white fox.

So Gordon ran back to Wise Owl's tree. He stood on his hind legs and scratched at the bark. "I need a rabbit!" he howled.

But Wise Owl wasn't there.

"Looking for someone?" A huge, fluffy rabbit popped his head out from under the tree. At first Gordon couldn't see him because his white fur was the same color as the snow. Also, the rabbit didn't come too close. He was a smart rabbit and his mother had always warned him about grizzly bears. *They may act sweet as pie, son, but when they're hungry, most of 'em forget their manners.*

Gordon stared at the rabbit's pink eyes and slowly made out his floppy ears and his fluffy tail. He was perfect!

"Pleased to meet you," cried Gordon. "I'm a magician and I'm looking for a rabbit!"

The rabbit cocked his head. "You

look like a grizzly bear to me."

"I'm a magician first and a grizzly bear second," said Gordon. He put his paw on his chest. "I promise."

The rabbit shot out from under the tree, did a full somersault, and landed on the ground. "Then count me in," he cried. "I've always wanted to be a magician's rabbit."

"Haven't you forgotten something?" A skunk appeared from behind a snowy bush. "Every great magician needs a manager. Especially a good manager like me." She wrapped her bushy black-and-white tail around her neck like a scarf and waited. "I'll help you put on a really amazing magic show."

Gordon and the rabbit stared at each other. "What makes you such a good manager?" Gordon asked the skunk at last.

The skunk smiled a knowing smile and drew an exclamation mark in the air with the tip of her tail. "Because no one ever says no to me!"

Gordon and the rabbit turned to each other again. All the animals in the forest knew about skunks. It was true. You didn't say no to them. Not unless you wanted to be sprayed with the worst smell in the whole world so that none of your friends would come near you again.

"Okay, it's a deal," said Gordon.

The skunk chuckled. "Don't worry, you won't regret it," she said.

Weeks went by and the skunk kept her word. Soon the magic show was the talk of the forest. While Gordon and the rabbit practiced amazing tricks, the skunk, whose name was Nelly, gave all the animals something to do. The moose made a huge sign.

The other grizzly bears helped to flatten the snow to make a clearing. At first the bears all said they were too sleepy, especially Gordon's sister, Gabby. But then Nelly had given them all a hard stare and swished her tail in a very dangerous way. After that, everyone did as they were told.

The night of the Midwinter Magic Show finally arrived. Wise Owl had shown the wolves and foxes how to build a stage out of ice blocks. Simon, the squirrel, had decorated it with some holly and red berries.

Gordon stood behind a huge snowy bush in his top hat and cloak. "What happens if no one likes my magic?"

he asked Nelly nervously.

Nelly smiled her knowing smile. "Just do what I say," she replied. "I have an excellent trick for you to do." Then she whispered in his ear.

As the moon rose, the animals took their places in the clearing.

"I've heard Gordon has a brand-new trick," said a moose.

"Me, too," said a deer.

"My Gordon can do *anything*," said Gordon's mom proudly.

"Gordon is a very smart young grizzly bear," agreed Wise Owl.

The pine tree branch curtains were pulled back and Nelly stood in the middle of the stage.

"Animals of the North!" she cried.
"Welcome to our MIDWINTER
MAGIC SHOW!" She stood back and
held out her arms. "Now may I present
Gordon the Amazing Magician!"

Suddenly, Gordon wasn't nervous anymore! He made his rabbit fly out of his hat, sail over the trees, and land back in his hat again. He made stars fall from the sky and juggled them like enormous diamonds. He made snow whirl around his feet like a tiny tornado.

All the animals were stunned. Not one of them had ever seen anything like it!

"And now for my last trick," cried Gordon. He smiled and turned to where Gabby was sitting in the back. "This one is especially for my sister, Gabby!"

Nelly banged two heavy sticks

together on a tree stump so that they sounded like drums.

Everyone got very excited!

What was going to happen next?

Gordon took off his cloak and held it out in front of him. Then he winked at Nelly and shouted, *"Abracadabra!"*

All the animals gasped. Gabby's eyes nearly popped out of her head.

In the middle of the stage was a huge, long table. And it was stacked with everyone's favorite food. There was a mountain of moss, fish, snakes, insects, nuts, acorns, and grass. But best of all, there was an enormous pile of honeycombs.

Especially for Gabby!

As Gordon bowed, all the animals clapped and cheered. Then Gabby stood up and walked onto the stage. She threw her arms around Gordon's neck and gave him a great big hug.

A huge grin spread across Gordon's face. It was the first time she had ever been really nice to him.

"Three cheers for Gordon!" cried Gabby. "He is the greatest Grizzly Bear Magician in the World!"

Then, as the full moon made the black sky turn light and the snow sparkle like silver, the Midwinter Magic Show came to an end and the Midwinter Feast began.

The animals cheered so loudly that Gordon had to bow again. He had never felt so happy in his life.

That night, the mountain of delicious food never ran out and the feast went on and on.

Everyone agreed that Gabby was right.

Gordon really was the greatest Grizzly Bear Magician in the World!

THE TIME
OF THE
WHITE FUR

Penny Dolan

Ookalik the hare was born when the rocky mountain was speckled with bright green moss and tiny star like flowers.

Ookalik and his two sisters huddled against the earth. Above them stretched the wide spring sky. Below them stretched the valley, where the pine trees grew.

By night, Mother Hare warmed her young with the heat of her own body. By day, she kept watch over them. "Do not worry if I run off," Mother Hare explained. "I will not be leaving you. I will be leading away danger."

So, when Fox appeared on the mountainside, or Eagle's shadow darkened the sky, Mother Hare jumped up and ran off. Her bobbing white tail lured enemies away from her three babies.

Before long, Mother Hare gently lifted the young hares out of their open burrow. Hop by hop, jump by jump, Ookalik and his sisters examined the world around them. In the distance, they saw other young hares playing on the mountainside.

Then, one day, Mother Hare called the three hares to her. "Listen, my little ones," she said. "You have much to learn. See that pale sun above you? It will grow into a midsummer sun. As the sun grows big and strong, so must you."

"Why?" asked little Ookalik.

"Once midsummer is over, the days grow shorter and darker. Before long, the Time of the White Fur will come. By then, you must be bold and smart enough to take care of yourselves. You will be babies no more."

"The Time of the White Fur?" said Ookalik. "What does that mean?"

"Silly! Don't you know? It's the time of the year when our fur turns white, of course!" his two sisters said bossily. They had been listening to other mountain hares chatting.

Ookalik stared at the speckled gray-brown fur on his back. "Will it happen soon?" he asked.

Mother Hare's eyes danced with laughter. "Not for a long time," she said. "But it is important to learn what I have to teach you before that hard time comes."

So Mother Hare set to work. She taught the three young hares how to find fresh green shoots to nibble.

She taught them
which plants
were good to
eat, and where
to find the
clearest pools
of water.

She taught them to race as fast
as the wind, too. "Your life may
depend on how fast you can run,"
she said.

She taught them the best hare
tricks: how to dart around the thorn
bushes, how to twist and turn and
double back as they ran, and how to
stay so still they would seem like the
stones around them.

"Remember," she said, "your fur is speckled gray like the rocks right now, so no enemy can see your hiding place. Then, once winter comes, your white fur will hide you while the land is white with snow."

Slowly, the sun grew warmer. It made the daytime longer. It made the nighttime shorter. Young Ookalik liked the night, because he loved to stare at the full moon. He thought he could see a strange figure on the silvery disk.

"Who is that on the moon?" he asked.

"That is Moon Dancer, the greatest hare of all," Mother Hare said. She told Ookalik how the magic hare had danced so well that he had jumped right up to the moon.

I wish I could jump like Moon Dancer, Ookalik thought as he leaped all over the mountain. Even when the midsummer sun came, shining all day and night, Ookalik danced, because he knew Moon Dancer was still there, hidden in the bright sky.

Then the season began to change. The sun was not so strong. The trees in the valley turned a dull, dark green. Mist came creeping over the rocks. Water filled the spaces where the flowers once peeped, and the moss turned brown.

"Beware!" Mother Hare told her children. "This is the Time of the Hunter."

One morning, men with guns stood at the foot of the hares' hill. Ookalik tried to do what his mother had done, and lure the enemies away. While his sisters crouched down by the rocks, Ookalik jumped up and tried to dart off.

Bang! A bullet whistled past. Down dived Ookalik, into the nearest hollow. He lay there trembling, licking the place where his gray fur was torn. Sometimes it was better to hide than to be brave.

Luckily, the hunters did not come any closer. They turned and walked toward the Long Lake. All that day, the ducks and geese flew much higher in the sky.

At last a time came when the sun hardly shone. The darkness grew longer. The pools of water were crusted with ice, and it was hard to find food.

"Now you must be extra careful, since there are hungry animals around," said Mother Hare. "Especially foxes."

One afternoon, as Ookalik raced across the mountain, two strange, young hares stood in his way. Their fur seemed to be covered in white frost.

"Pleased to meet you," Ookalik said politely.

"It's only us, silly!" laughed his sisters, showing him the pale fur that lay across their backs. In a week their fur had become totally white. Ookalik stared at his own fur. It was still speckled gray.

White feathers of snow began to fall from the sky. Hour after hour they fell. The rough, rocky land was covered in soft, shining whiteness.

So this is the Time of the White Fur, Ookalik thought.

As he headed back to his burrow to find his mother, he noticed that all the other hares were covered in white fur. "Mother, what should I do?" he asked when he reached her.

"Don't worry, Ookalik. Keep out of sight. It will happen," Mother Hare told him. "Sometimes it just takes a while."

One morning, Ookalik awoke to find the world covered in white. Now he was in great danger. Anyone could spot a gray hare moving across the white mountain. So Ookalik burrowed himself down among the drifts of snow and hid for a long time. He did not mind the dark, but he did miss seeing his hero, Moon Dancer. One night the little hare could bear it no longer. Ookalik poked his nose above the snow.

He could not see Moon Dancer, but he did see the magical lights rippling across the sky, shining red and green and blue and gold.

They flickered and gleamed, whirling and changing as if the wind itself was alight. The whole sky shimmered. Transfixed, Ookalik watched the lights dance above the wonderful whiteness of the snow.

"Grrrr! Got you, hare!" Something pounced, something with sharp teeth and a terrible scent on its rough fur. Fox!

Ookalik jumped so high that the cruel mouth snapped and missed its bite.

Ookalik began to run, twisting this way and that way. His ears lay back. His strong feet beat on the ground. *Thump, thump, thump!* He could feel his own heart thudding wildly. He could feel the hot breath close behind him.

"Moon Dancer, save me!" he cried.

Down the mountainside raced Ookalik. Blindly, he ran into the valley. He saw the shadowy snow beneath the trees. Wouldn't he be safer there? But Fox was still behind him. *Go, Ookalik, go!*

An old log cabin stood under the trees. A narrow rectangle of light appeared. Ookalik ran toward it, darting between the feet of a man and a boy who were struggling to get inside with a small tree. The hare pushed through the scented branches, and disappeared into the darkness beneath a cupboard. He squeezed himself into the corner and closed his eyes in fear.

Fox was scrabbling at the metal step, but the man was shouting, using his boots and a stick to drive the enemy away. Ookalik heard a slamming sound, and realized he was trapped inside the cabin.

He shivered as a flashlight beam washed over him. A boy was kneeling down, looking closely.

"Something did run under here, Dad," he said, then gasped. "It's a young hare!"

"Well, the poor thing won't hurt us. It'll come out when it's good and ready," the man said. "Come on, let's get our tree set up now that we've brought it home."

From his dark hiding place, Ookalik heard songs being played softly. He heard the man and boy chatting, wrapping things in paper, and laughing. He smelled the forest scent of the tree, and the good things the man and boy were munching. Finally, the boy yawned and the father yawned.

"Bedtime!" said the man, laughing. The boy climbed into a bunk. The man went off to his own room.

"Good night, little hare," said the boy.

Ookalik's night seemed to go on forever. When it was all quiet at last, he hopped out.

There in front of him stood the tree, but something had happened. The green branches were hung with round, silver balls, each one shining like a moon. Entranced, the little hare hopped closer and closer. There was something familiar about the beautiful silver globes.

Then Ookalik sat up in surprise. He jumped this way and that way, his head to one side. What had he seen? There, inside each moon-like shape he saw a hare, a magical hare, dancing and swaying. It must be Moon Dancer, come to help him!

Strangely, his hero's fur was not pure white, but a soft silvery white. The little hare gazed at the tree.

Then Ookalik heard a soft noise behind him. As he turned his head and saw the young boy standing there, he also saw his own fur. It had changed, too! His fur was the same color as Moon Dancer's!

"Hello there, little hare! Merry Christmas!" the boy said. "Should I let you out now?"

Then the boy opened the cabin door, and the winter wind outside seemed to call a name. *Ookalik!*

The little hare glanced once again at Moon Dancer's tree. Then he leaped out through the door and danced back across the snow to where the other hares were waiting in their white winter fur.

SEAL
BROTHER

Elizabeth Baguley

Lights shone through the Arctic darkness from the windows of a low, stone house. It was Christmas Eve, and inside, a mother was hanging the last ornament on a Christmas tree. She turned to her son, who was hugging his knees as he sat on the floor, staring at a cream-colored disk held in his hand. In the lamplight, his pale hair looked gray and his dark eyes had the soft glimmer of ice.

"Euan! You aren't listening to me!" teased his mother. "I said, why don't you help me light the candles on the tree?" She smiled at him. He hadn't heard her asking him about the lights. His mind wasn't on the tree with its winking tinsel. He was thinking about the sea, as always.

Euan held the cream disk tightly. It was a whalebone on which Father had carved a picture of his fishing boat, the *Midnight Sun*. When Father went away to sea on a fishing trip, he would always give Euan the little carving, saying to him, "Keep the *Midnight Sun* safe for me, and I'll be home safe soon!"

And this time he'd added, "Keep it safe until Christmas—that's when I'll be back!"

So Euan kept the whalebone close, like a lucky charm, so that his father would return from the rough Arctic Ocean for the tree and Christmas dinner and presents.

Now it was Christmas Eve, and Euan only had to keep the whalebone safe for a few more hours until his father came home.

"Let's light the candles on the tree now," said Mother, louder than before, "and then when your father comes, he'll see them through the window."

But Euan still wasn't listening to her. His ears were filled with the heavy drumming of the sea, rolling and crashing over the rocks in the bay. He heard the wolf-howl of the wind—and through all this noise came the sound of a seal crying.

"There's snow on the way," Euan said to his mother. "Heavy snow."

"Are the seals telling you?" she asked.

"It's Oogruq. She's calling from the beach."

Euan's mother nodded. Although she couldn't understand the seals' cries herself, her son always seemed to know what they were saying.

He dreamed of the sea and loved the seals like brothers and sisters— especially Oogruq.

The year before, Euan had found a baby seal on the beach. She had a ripped flipper and was yelping in pain. He had fed her and bathed her wound until one day she had slipped into the waves, all better again. Euan had watched the small seal go, hardly believing that she was big enough to swim across the endless ocean all the way to the Arctic and back. He had named her Oogruq, which meant *seal* in the language of the North. She would always call to him when she came to the beach. This time her cry warned him of danger out at sea.

Euan frowned. Oogruq was crying, "Danger! Snow!" Her voice was high and loud above the wolf-wind—she was warning him as loudly as she could. Euan knew the snowstorm was speeding toward the bay faster than a small fishing boat could travel over water. The *Midnight Sun* might be lost in the storm.

"Don't worry," Mother said, seeing her son's anxious face, "the *Midnight Sun* is nearly back. Daddy said so on the radio. He'll be in the bay before bedtime."

Euan hurried toward the door.

"Euan, where are you going?" Mother asked.

"To the bay," he said, "to watch for Daddy." Mother didn't stop him. It was as if the sea was pulling him toward it, so that he had to go. She helped him into his outdoor clothes, so thick they made him almost round. His legs looked short and his hands in their thick gloves were as stumpy as flippers.

Out he went into the cold. Cold? It was worse than cold. A snarling wind bullied him as he pushed against it over the stony path. It was Christmas Eve. The air should have been full of shimmer and excitement. There should have been carols around the Christmas tree and the smell of roasting meat and spiced cider. But the storm didn't understand that. It had ripped the sea and the sky into little pieces and was throwing them around in a wild battle in the bay. No boat could come through this in one piece.

Euan gripped the whalebone tightly. "I'm keeping you safe," he said, both to the carving and to his father. "Please be safe!"

He knelt down on the rocky shore near the harbor where the boats pulled against their ropes, tugged at by the tide. Oogruq was high up the beach. Euan stretched out his hand to her and she shuffled to get close to him. The young seal was pleased to see Euan and leaned heavily against his legs. Then she barked, telling of snow, storm, and sea swell.

"My father's in danger," Euan said to her. "His boat is out there— and here comes the snow!"

Over the sea it swept, a white monster of a storm. It was so thick Euan couldn't see the water at all.

"He won't be able to see the rocks!" Euan cried, thinking of the way his father always wove the boat in and out of the sharp rocks in the bay as he steered into the harbor. Father knew the rocks almost as well as the seals did; he knew where each one lay and he knew its name. The rocks all had names: Shark's Tooth, Splinter Rock, the Smasher. They waited to chew up boats thrown against them in a storm.

Euan showed Oogruq the whalebone with its carving of the *Midnight Sun*. Perhaps she could help him stop the boat from coming into the harbor somehow.

"What are you doing?" he shouted suddenly. The seal had taken the whalebone from his hand and before he could snatch it back, she had dived into the water.

"Come back!" he yelled. "I have to keep that safe. I have to keep my father safe!"

But Father wasn't safe now. No matter how hard Euan looked, he couldn't see the small seal.

How could she keep the whalebone in her mouth when she was rolled and rocked by such huge waves? The lucky charm wouldn't still be lucky if it fell to the bottom of the sea. He began to cry, the tears stinging his cheeks. He should never have come here alone. He should never have brought the whalebone with him, or shown it to Oogruq. She must have thought he was playing with her. She was too young to understand how important the whalebone was to him.

Then he saw something through his tears and through the shifting walls of snow. Thrown up and down on the plunging waves, there was a boat out in the bay. It tipped and tilted, pushed forward by the wind. Euan recognized it. It was the bravest boat ever. It was the *Midnight Sun*—and on it, though he was too far away to see, was Daddy. The boat was heading for Shark's Tooth, Splinter Rock, and the Smasher. And in the blinding snow, his father couldn't see them. He wouldn't be able to steer the brave little boat and bring it safely into the harbor.

"I've lost the whalebone!" he shouted to his father over the wind. "Go back! Don't come into the bay!"

His father was almost home, but the ship would be splintered and smashed. There was nothing he could do to help, and it was all his fault.

Huge sobs burst from him, and wouldn't stop. His voice sounded croaky and loud—a horrible, painful bark.

Then something was barking back. Above the drumming crash and roll of the sea and the wolf-howl of the wind, a seal was barking at him. This time it wasn't a danger call: It was the cry that Oogruq always made when she was coming to the beach.

Euan climbed up onto the harbor wall, clinging to a rope for safety. From here, he could see the

Midnight Sun rising and falling. The rocks jutted their sharp teeth toward the little boat. Euan held his breath. But suddenly he caught sight of a shiny gray seal's head, like a silver light in the water. Oogruq swam one way then the other, weaving a path between the rocks, and Euan watched as the *Midnight Sun* followed. Oogruq was the eyes of the brave boat, guiding his father to safety.

Euan found himself crying again, but this time not from sadness. He felt so proud of the little seal. Eagerly, he watched the boat lurch into the harbor, rescued from danger by Oogruq. Euan didn't know who to hug first as his father and the seal came onto dry land. They were both part of his family and he loved them with all his heart.

In the stone house, the candles on the Christmas tree shone. It was Christmas Eve. Meat was roasting and the fire was warm. Father was carving the face of a large-eyed, fine-whiskered seal on the other side of the whalebone, to remind everyone who saw it that Oogruq had saved the *Midnight Sun* from being dashed on the rocks.

Euan opened the door of the small stone cottage and whispered toward the bay. He needed to say something before it was time to open the Christmas presents.

"Merry Christmas, Oogruq, and thank you for the best Christmas gift of all!" he said, hoping she could understand him.

And Oogruq, her voice full of love, called back, "Merry Christmas, Seal Brother."